P9-DOB-687

Dear Parents:

Congratulations! Your child is taking the first steps on an exciting journey. The destination? Independent reading!

STEP INTO READING® will help your child get there. The program offers five steps to reading success. Each step includes fun stories and colorful art or photographs. In addition to original fiction and books with favorite characters, there are Step into Reading Non-Fiction Readers, Phonics Readers and Boxed Sets, Sticker Readers, and Comic Readers—a complete literacy program with something to interest every child.

Learning to Read, Step by Step!

Ready to Read   Preschool–Kindergarten
• big type and easy words • rhyme and rhythm • picture clues
For children who know the alphabet and are eager to begin reading.

Reading with Help   Preschool–Grade 1
• basic vocabulary • short sentences • simple stories
For children who recognize familiar words and sound out new words with help.

Reading on Your Own   Grades 1–3
• engaging characters • easy-to-follow plots • popular topics
For children who are ready to read on their own.

Reading Paragraphs   Grades 2–3
• challenging vocabulary • short paragraphs • exciting stories
For newly independent readers who read simple sentences with confidence.

Ready for Chapters   Grades 2–4
• chapters • longer paragraphs • full-color art
For children who want to take the plunge into chapter books but still like colorful pictures.

STEP INTO READING® is designed to give every child a successful reading experience. The grade levels are only guides; children will progress through the steps at their own speed, developing confidence in their reading.

Remember, a lifetime love of reading starts with a single step!

Copyright © 2022 Disney Enterprises, Inc. and Pixar. All rights reserved. Published in the United States by Random House Children's Books, a division of Penguin Random House LLC, 1745 Broadway, New York, NY 10019, and in Canada by Penguin Random House Canada Limited, Toronto, in conjunction with Disney Enterprises, Inc.

Step into Reading, Random House, and the Random House colophon are registered trademarks of Penguin Random House LLC.

Visit us on the Web!
StepIntoReading.com
rhcbooks.com

Educators and librarians, for a variety of teaching tools, visit us at RHTeachersLibrarians.com

ISBN 978-0-7364-4294-7 (trade) — ISBN 978-0-7364-9013-9 (lib. bdg.)
ISBN 978-0-7364-4295-4 (ebook)

Printed in the United States of America

10 9 8 7 6 5 4 3 2 1

Random House Children's Books supports the First Amendment and celebrates the right to read.

DISNEY · PIXAR

Space Ranger
to the Rescue

adapted by Natasha Bouchard

illustrated by the Disney Storybook Art Team

Random House 🏠 New York

Space Ranger Buzz Lightyear and his commander, Alisha, are exploring a new planet.

Suddenly, giant bugs
and vines attack them!
Buzz, Alisha, and their crew
escape to their ship.
Buzz struggles to launch it.
He does not want any help.
He crashes the ship!

The crash destroys
the hyperspeed fuel crystal.
Without it, their ship
cannot take them home.
They are stranded!

Buzz wants to fix his mistake.
He will test a new
fuel-crystal formula
on a different ship.
Airman Díaz prepares Buzz
for the flight.

The ship launches.

Buzz increases the ship's speed.

But the fuel crystal is unstable.

The ship loses power.

Buzz lands the ship.

The new fuel-crystal formula

does not work.

The mission has failed.

Díaz welcomes Buzz back.

But Díaz is now four years older.

The faster Buzz flies,

the further he travels

into the future.

His friends grow older.

But Buzz stays the same age.

Buzz asks Sox, his robot cat,
to help him solve the
fuel-crystal formula problem.

Buzz returns from

another failed mission.

Now Alisha is much older.

She has a grandchild named Izzy.

Izzy wants to be a Space Ranger.

Alisha sends Buzz

a farewell message.

She still believes in Buzz.

She encourages him

to finish his mission.

But the mission gets shut down.

Everyone will stay on the planet.

Then Sox the robot cat creates

the right fuel-crystal formula!

Buzz thinks they should

complete the mission.

Buzz and Sox use the new
fuel-crystal formula
to launch a ship.
They reach hyperspeed.
Buzz finally completes
the mission!

Buzz and Sox land their ship . . .

twenty-two years in the future!

Alien robots have invaded the planet.

Izzy, now all grown up, finds Buzz.

They watch an alien robot tap

his ship with a transport disc.

The ship disappears.

Izzy introduces Buzz
to her friends Mo and Darby.
They need Buzz's help
to defeat the alien robots
and pilot a ship.

Buzz agrees to join their team.

Suddenly, an alien robot appears

and grabs Buzz.

Izzy, Mo, and Darby
clumsily defeat the robot.
Buzz realizes they are
not trained Space Rangers.

Buzz wants to continue

the mission alone.

But he also needs their help

in navigating the planet.

Now they are a team, and they

launch a new ship.

Zurg, the leader
of the alien robots,
chases them.
The team's ship crash-lands!

Zurg's ship continues its attack.

The team runs from their ship!

Zurg follows them.

He traps Buzz in a corner.

Darby saves Buzz just in time!

The team boards their damaged
ship, but it can only hover.
Sox repairs it while
alien robots chase the ship
through some lava fields.

Sox has fixed the ship!
But Izzy makes a mistake,
and the ship crashes again.
An alien robot snatches
the fuel crystal
and takes it
to Zurg's ship.

Zurg grabs Buzz

and presses a transport disc

on his suit.

They teleport to Zurg's ship!

Zurg plans to use the crystal
to travel back in time.
He will change the past.
Everything will be different.
Buzz thinks it is a bad idea.
Doing that would erase Izzy
and Alisha's family.

Buzz realizes their lives
are more important
than fixing his mistake.

Buzz battles Zurg, and

the team arrives to save Buzz.

Buzz needs their help!

Izzy tosses Buzz

his wrist blaster.

Buzz fires his wrist blaster at
the self-destruct button
on Zurg's ship.
The team escapes
with the fuel crystal.
Zurg's ship explodes!

Buzz is sucked into space.

Suddenly, Zurg appears!

He grabs the fuel crystal.

Buzz blasts it away.

The fuel crystal is destroyed.

Now the ship is about to crash!
Buzz and the team work together
to safely land on the planet.
At last, the planet is free
from Zurg and the alien robots.

Now they're all Space Rangers:

Buzz, Izzy, Mo, and Darby.

They will protect the galaxy—

to infinity . . . and beyond!